HELPING YOUR BRAND-NEW READER

Here's how to make first-time reading easy and fun:

▶ Read the introduction at the beginning of each story aloud. Look through the pictures together so that your child can see what happens in the story before reading the words.

▶ Read the first page to your child, placing your finger under each word.

▶ Let your child touch the words and read the rest of the story. Give him or her time to figure out each new word.

▶ If your child gets stuck on a word, you might say, *"Try something. Look at the picture. What would make sense?"*

▶ If your child is still stuck, supply the right word. This will allow him or her to continue to read and enjoy the story. You might say, *"Could this word be 'ball'?"*

▶ Always praise your child. Praise what he or she reads correctly, and praise good tries too.

▶ Give your child lots of chances to read the story again and again. The more your child reads, the more confident he or she will become.

▶ Have fun!

First edition 2002

Library of Congress Cataloging-in-Publication Data

Root, Phyllis.
Mouse goes out / Phyllis Root ;
illustrated by James Croft. — 1st ed.
p.   cm. — (Brand new readers)
Summary: As the seasons change, Mouse tries fishing,
making a snowman, swimming, and camping.
ISBN 0-7636-1351-7
[1. Mice—Fiction. 2. Seasons—Fiction. 3. Fishing—Fiction.
4. Snowmen—Fiction. 5. Rain and rainfall—Fiction.
6. Camping—Fiction.] I. Croft, James, ill. II. Title. III. Series.
PZ7.R6784   Mp 2002
[E]—dc21   2001047022

2 4 6 8 10 9 7 5 3 1

Printed in Hong Kong

This book was typeset in Letraset Arta.
The illustrations were done in acrylic and pastel.

Candlewick Press
2067 Massachusetts Avenue
Cambridge, Massachusetts 02140

visit us at www.candlewick.com

MOUSE
GOES OUT

CANDLEWICK PRESS
CAMBRIDGE, MASSACHUSETTS

Phyllis Root ILLUSTRATED BY **James Croft**

Contents

PUDDLES

Introduction

This story is called *Puddles*.
It's about how Mouse keeps jumping
in puddles and gets his shoes, pants,
and shirt wet. Then he jumps in a big
puddle — and swims!

3

Mouse jumps in a puddle.

4

Mouse gets his boots wet.

5

Mouse jumps in a puddle.

6

Mouse gets his pants wet.

Mouse jumps in a puddle.

8

Mouse gets his shirt wet.

9

Mouse jumps in a **BIG** puddle.

10

Mouse swims.

THE BIG FISH

Introduction

This story is called *The Big Fish*.
It's about how Mouse goes fishing
and catches a boot, a stick, and a fish,
and throws them back into the water.
Then Mouse catches a big fish, who
throws Mouse back.

13

Mouse catches a boot.

14

Mouse throws the boot back.

Mouse catches a stick.

16

Mouse throws the stick back.

17

Mouse catches a fish.

Mouse throws the fish back.

19

Mouse catches a BIG fish.

The big fish throws Mouse back.

CAMPING

Introduction

This story is called *Camping*.
It's about how Mouse camps in the woods.
But when he sees a tail and eyes and teeth,
he gets scared and camps in his house.

23

Mouse camps in the woods.

24

Mouse sleeps.

25

Mouse wakes up.

Mouse sees a tail.

27

Mouse sees eyes.

28

Mouse sees more eyes.

Mouse sees teeth.

30

Mouse camps in his house.

SNOW MOUSE

31

Introduction

This story is called *Snow Mouse*.
It's about how Mouse makes snowballs
and then takes off his hat, coat, scarf,
and mittens to make a snowman
in the shape of a mouse.

Mouse makes a snowball.

Mouse makes another snowball.

Mouse makes more snowballs.

36

Mouse takes off his hat.

37

Mouse takes off his coat.

38

Mouse takes off his scarf.

39

Mouse takes off his mittens.

40

Hello, Snow Mouse!